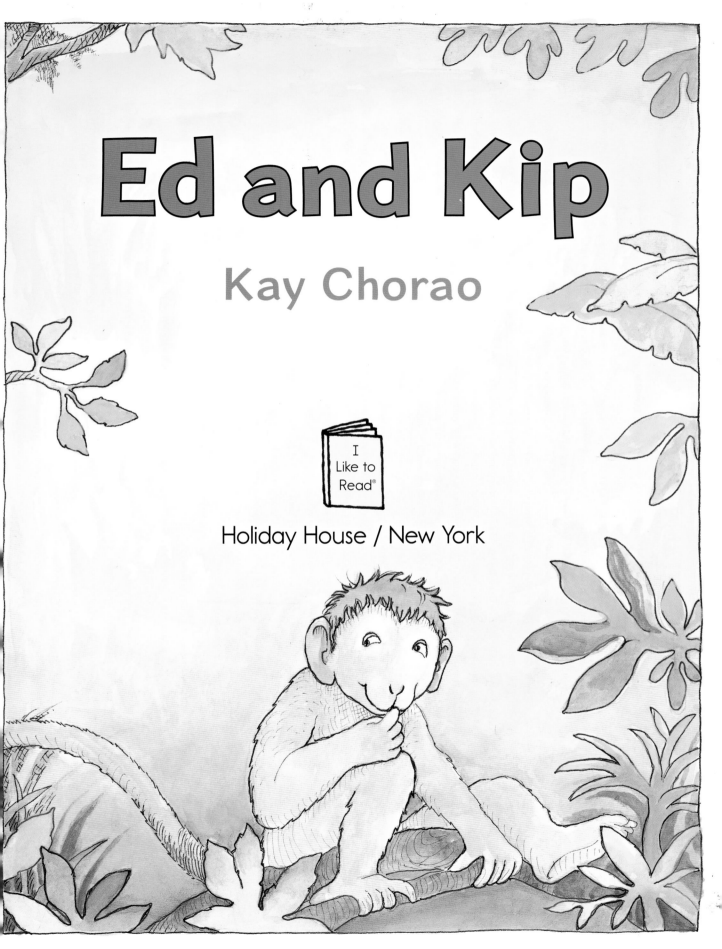

Ed and Kip

Kay Chorao

I Like to Read®

Holiday House / New York

For Sadie, who has been known to play with bugs

I LIKE TO READ is a registered trademark of Holiday House, Inc.
Copyright © 2014 by Kay Chorao
All Rights Reserved
HOLIDAY HOUSE is registered in the U.S. Patent and Trademark Office.
Printed and Bound in November 2013 at Tien Wah Press, Johor Bahru, Johor Malaysia.
The text typeface is Report School.
The artwork was created with watercolor, gouache, and ink on 140 lb. hot press watercolor paper.
www.holidayhouse.com
First Edition
1 3 5 7 9 10 8 6 4 2

Library of Congress Cataloging-in-Publication Data
Chorao, Kay.
Ed and Kip / Kay Chorao. — First edition.
pages cm. — (I like to read)
Summary: Elephants Ed and Kip play with a rolling rock.
ISBN 978-0-8234-2903-5 (hardcover)
[1. Elephants—Fiction. 2. Play—Fiction. 3. Rocks—Fiction. 4. Jungle animals—Fiction.] I. Title.
PZ7.C4463Ed 2014
[E]—dc23
2012045920

Monkey dropped a rock.

Ed rolled it to Kip.

It rolled out.

Can we play?

Ed rolled the rock to Bug.

You will play with me?

Bug rolled it back.
It rolled far.

Splash!

Ed and Kip slid down.

A big head came up.

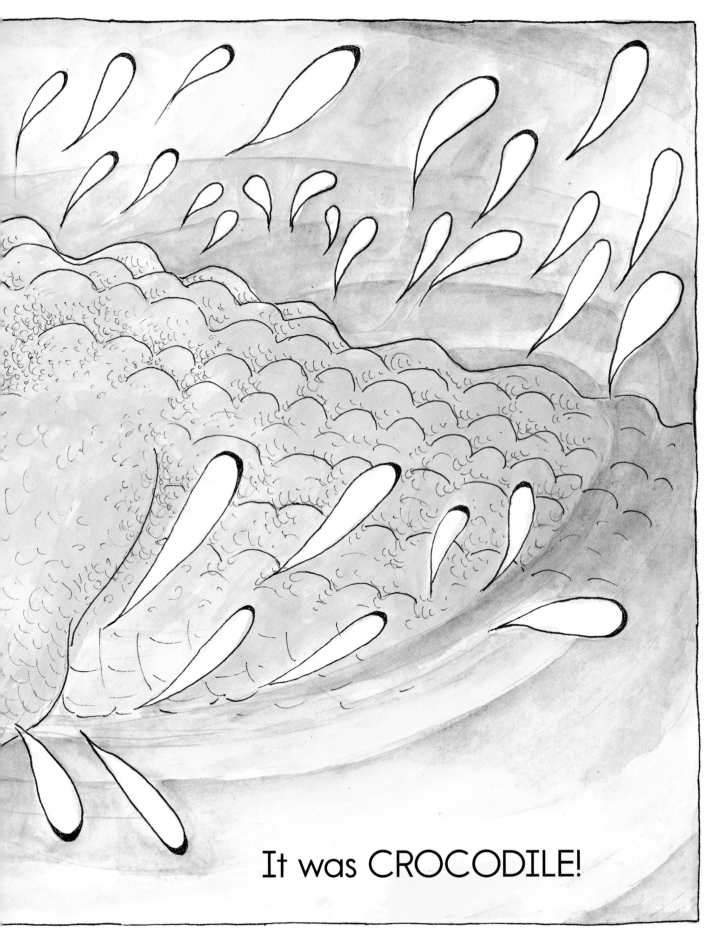

It was CROCODILE!

Ed and Kip were scared.

Crocodile opened wide.

In jumped
Bug.

He poked.

He bit.

Crocodile was surprised.

Bug jumped out.

Crocodile
watched Bug.

Ed and Kip threw in the rock.

Ed and Kip ran home.
Bug rode.

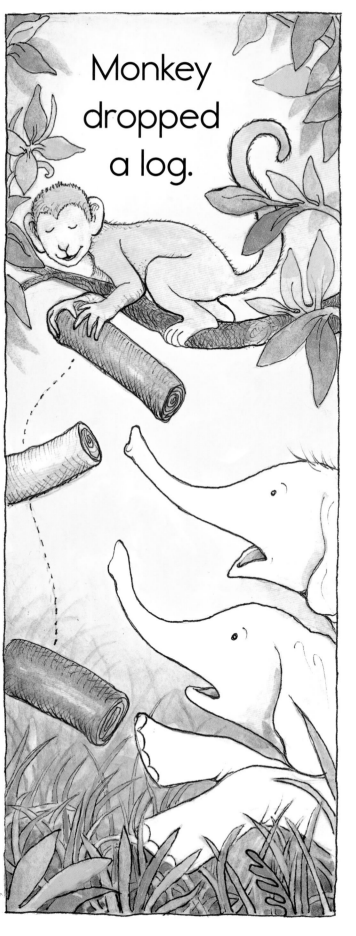